A CHRISTMAS MENAGERIE

A CHRISTMAS MENAGERIE

A Scary, Merry Anthology of Heartwarming Horror

KEITH SIMPKINS

© 2025 Drill Down Publishing LLC. All rights reserved.

No part of this book may be reproduced, stored, or transmitted in any form or by any means—electronic, mechanical, photocopying, recording, or otherwise—without the prior written permission of the publisher, except for brief excerpts used in reviews or as permitted by law.

First published in 2025 by:
Drill Down Publishing LLC
Mentor, OH

Publisher contact:
PO Box 1687
Mentor, OH 44061
info@drilldownpublishing.com

ISBN (Hardcover): 979-8-9921126-0-3
ISBN (Paperback): 979-8-9921126-1-0
ISBN (eBook): 979-8-9921126-2-7

Library of Congress Control Number: 2025921648

A Winter's Night Tale

A CHRISTMAS MENAGERIE

A cold wind swept across the field as a nearly full moon hung in the sky. The night was so crisp and clean that it felt like the entire universe was on display. A fresh blanket of snow had fallen, adding to the beauty of the night as the bare tree branches clattered together in the wind.

It was a night that just felt like Christmas.

At the edge of the field, a cozy house sat dark, its family long ago fallen asleep. The Christmas tree twinkled in the darkness, waiting for the family to wake up and gather around its branches to open the mounds of gifts stacked beneath them. Each package was wrapped in an array of dazzling colors, topped with intricately tied bows and cards displaying names in perfect calligraphy.

On a small table next to the empty fireplace sat a plate of cookies and a glass of milk, waiting for the most special guest to arrive. Next to the milk sat a note scrawled in a child's hand that said:

Dear Santa,
Here is a small snack for your journey tonight.
I have been a good boy this year.
Enjoy the cookies.
Merry Christmas and love,
Henry
P.S. I really would love a bike for Christmas.

A WINTER'S NIGHT TALE

Up the stairs and on the left was the bedroom of young Henry. Inside, he lay asleep dreaming of all the wonderful toys he would play with in the morning. Down the hall was the bedroom of Henry's parents, Jim and Linda, both sleeping soundly after assembling all the toys for their son's Christmas morning. Jim snored lightly as Linda rolled to her other side, drifting deeper into sleep.

A loud thump on the roof shook the house as Henry dozed peacefully. He stirred, mumbled, and grabbed his stuffed bunny before drifting back to sleep. Footsteps and a dragging sound could be heard on the roof, followed by something sliding down the chimney. With a grunt and a few moans, a figure emerged from the fireplace and set his sack close to the tree.

As he stood up, he took in the sight of the majestic Christmas tree before him and uttered a soft "Ho, Ho, Ho." Twinkling lights cast a gentle glow, illuminating branches adorned with ornaments from Jim and Linda's childhoods and a cherished memento of little Henry's first Christmas. The tree stood proudly as a living museum of the small family's life together.

Garland in red, the color of pomegranates, wound through the branches, wrapping them like fine jewelry and leading to the top of the tree, where a Santa tree topper sat. This was no ordinary Santa tree topper. This Santa wore the finest Laplander garb, including a long, flowing red robe trimmed with the finest brown coyote fur. His boots were black as midnight on the winter solstice, and his deep pine-green

4

A CHRISTMAS MENAGERIE

pants complemented a red shirt adorned with shiny black buttons and a soft white fur collar. His face was framed by a curly beard as white as freshly fallen snow, and a red hat trimmed in the same fur as his robe sat atop his head. He held a staff topped with a lantern in his right hand while his left hand gently rested on a reindeer seated at his side. As the figure fixed his gaze on the sight of the tree topper, a warmth filled his eyes, and a soft smile stretched across his mouth.

Strung across the fireplace were three stockings with the names Mom, Dad, and Henry intricately stitched across the top. To its left sat an old, dark brown leather chair. This used to be the prized seat in the house – a spot that Henry always loved. Sitting on his father's lap, he would listen to stories from the numerous books on the shelves behind the chair. It had been his escape from the world for the briefest of moments.

Beside the chair stood the small table bearing a plate of cookies, a glass of milk, and the note from little Henry. The figure picked up the note and read the words Henry had scrawled on it, his eyes narrowing as he reached the last line. A hint of amusement flickered across his face as he turned back to the tree, unknowingly bumping the table and causing it to slide across the floor.

Upstairs, Henry was pulled from his slumber when he heard the table scrape on the living room floor. Sitting upright in his bed as quietly as he could, he held his breath and strained to listen for any trace of sound. To his astonishment, a small "Ho, Ho, Ho" drifted up from downstairs, causing his pulse to

5

beat like a bass drum in his chest at the thought of Santa being in his living room.

Henry quietly peeled back the covers, then slowly swung his legs over the side of the bed and eased onto the floor. He held his breath as he took a step across the floor, only letting it out when his foot was firmly planted on the ground. It felt like hours stretched by as he moved delicately to the door, though it only took a few seconds. He carefully turned the doorknob and opened the door just enough to squeeze through.

Downstairs, the figure pulled his sack towards him and, as he did so, made another slight scraping noise. Thinking nothing of it, he opened his sack and bent over, peering inside and moving the contents around as if looking for something in particular. Occasionally, he would look up and chuckle softly while rummaging around. At one point, the figure paused, thinking he heard something upstairs, but when no further sound came, he continued his work.

Once outside his bedroom, Henry stopped and listened, hearing faint sounds of someone moving things around and laughing. He excitedly crept towards the stairs, trying not to make a sound. The living room was situated in such a way that it couldn't be seen from the top landing, so he sat down on the first step to listen and make sure he was not heard. Nothing... so he slid to the next step, then the next step.

Henry made it to the next landing, where he could see the big leather chair he used to love beside the fireplace. From there, he could barely make out the shape of someone next to

A CHRISTMAS MENAGERIE

the tree. Moving even more cautiously, Henry inched down the remaining steps, one at a time, pausing at each one to make sure he wasn't heard. At the bottom, he carefully peered around the banister to see a mound of a figure garbed in a red robe trimmed in coyote fur, with black boots peering out from under its hem. Henry could not believe his eyes. Before him stood *the* Santa – his dreams had come true, and Santa had come to visit him.

The figure was still stooped over his sack when he heard the softest of scrapings coming down the stairs. A grin spread across his face – this must be young Henry, sneaking down to spy on him. He didn't quicken his pace nor try to hide; instead, he let Henry believe he had gone unnoticed, busying himself as the boy descended the remaining steps. As Henry quietly exclaimed, "Santa!" the figure started to stand up.

Henry excitedly stood his ground, waiting to see Santa's face beaming at him. He was so thrilled that he almost forgot what he had asked for. As the figure rose to his full height and began to turn towards Henry, the hood of his robe fell back, revealing his red and fur-trimmed Santa hat. Finally facing Henry, the figure slowly lifted his head.

Henry's eyes were wide from the shock of spying upon Santa in his living room. His mind raced with everything he wanted to say and the gifts he would get – until something cut through his visions. It was Santa's laugh, but somehow different than he was expecting. Something was not right. The dark face leering at him had a dirty grey beard wrapped around a pointy chin. The eyes staring into young Henry's soul were black as

A WINTER'S NIGHT TALE

pitch. A long, sharp red tongue slid from a mouth framed by rows of sharp, pointed teeth, licking his lips before he deeply intoned, "Hennnnn-reeeee…"

Henry's excitement turned to terror as he took in the figure before him. Thinking that he surely must be dreaming, he tried to shake himself awake, but the figure just laughed at his floundering. Next, he tried to back away, but his feet were frozen with fear. His mind couldn't seem to do anything but focus on the shape in front of him. How could this be? Santa was supposed to be a jolly man, round and jovial, but this… this was terrifying beyond belief. The figure moved towards Henry, seemingly gliding across the floor without moving his legs. The closer it got, the more fear Henry felt, but he still could not move.

The figure stretched out his arm towards Henry, the appendage ending in what could only be described as a claw. Although it resembled a hand in that it had five digits, each one curled unnaturally and came to a point with a sharp nail. Seeing the hand move closer to his face, Henry wanted to turn and run or disappear from this very spot, but neither happened. He stood there, terrified and unable to utter a sound, until the claw wrapped around his shoulder. The touch sent a shock through Henry's body, and suddenly his mind was overrun with vivid images.

A CHRISTMAS MENAGERIE

A movie started playing in Henry's mind, casting him as the main character in a scene set in the living room earlier that year. He had been playing with his toys while his father was at work and his mother was cooking dinner in the kitchen. On the fireplace mantel sat his mother's prized possession: a porcelain doll that her mother had given her before she died. Thinking it would be the perfect damsel in distress for his toy castle, Henry perched the doll in the tower keep and surrounded it with dragons, trolls, and other small toys to protect it from invaders. Next, he grabbed his favorite toy, Batman, and mounted him on the back of a horse. As Batman stormed the castle, Henry got carried away in the heat of battle and accidentally knocked the fragile doll to the floor.

As it hit the floor, the doll broke into pieces – the head came off at the shoulders, and the body broke in half at the waist. Each was a clean break, almost perfect. When his mother heard the crash, she rushed in to investigate and found Henry seated in front of his toys with the broken porcelain doll on the floor near the hearth. Devastated, she asked Henry what had happened.

With a look of confusion and fear, Henry stammered that the cat had jumped onto the mantel and knocked it off, pointing at the patsy grooming itself in the leather chair. His mother looked at him incredulously and asked again, "What happened?" Once more, he insisted it was the cat; it had leaped onto the mantel, knocked the doll to the floor, and then settled on the chair to lie down. Seeing the sadness and fear in his eyes, she reluctantly believed him and threw the cat outside.

9

A WINTER'S NIGHT TALE

The scene changed before Henry could process what he was seeing. Suddenly, it was early summer, and he was outside where his cat kept pestering him as he tried to play. Aggravated that it wouldn't leave him alone, he pushed it away, wishing his mother had gotten rid of it when she thought it had knocked over her doll. The cat looked at Henry lovingly and chittered at him softly. Thinking the cat was mocking him, he grabbed it by the scruff of the neck and tried to shove it into a sack lying close by as it growled and hissed at him.

"Hey, Henry, stop! You're hurting that kitty," he heard from the edge of his yard. Looking up, he saw Sally from next door staring straight at him. "Leave that kitty alone, or I'll tell your mommy," she chided.

As Henry told her to mind her own business and turned to walk away, Sally began yelling for his mother. He whirled around and shouted, "FINE!" before opening the bag to let the cat out. "I wasn't going to hurt it; I was only playing," he insisted before begging Sally not to tell on him.

The scene changed again. This time, Henry was at school on the playground, where the children laughed and enjoyed themselves during their break from the classroom. Sally stood in the middle of the playground, chatting with her friends and showing off her new dress as they complimented her. While Sally was well-liked at school, Henry made excuses for his lack of friends. He convinced himself that Sally bribed kids to befriend her and invited them over to flaunt her family's wealth and all her new toys. It often made Henry feel like a poor kid no one wanted to be around.

10

A CHRISTMAS MENAGERIE

When the bell rang to signal the end of recess, everyone started moving back towards the school. Sally lingered to collect her bag, telling her friends she'd meet them inside. Unnoticed, Henry watched her from behind a tree, his eyes following her every move. As she walked back towards the building, she noticed a large mud puddle and carefully tried to walk around it. Suddenly, she felt a strong push from behind, and before she knew what had happened, she was engulfed in its cold, thick embrace. She tried to scream, but as she opened her mouth, it was filled with a dirty-tasting liquid. Gagging, she spat it out as quickly as she could. As she rolled around in the mud, Henry's laughter echoed behind her as he ran in the opposite direction.

Two minutes later, the teacher came looking for Sally and found her crying in the mud. When the teacher asked what had happened, all Sally could say was that it felt like someone had pushed her down hard. She hadn't seen who it was, but in her heart, she was sure it had to be Henry. She tried to tell the teacher, but her teacher dismissed the idea, explaining that Henry was in the classroom and had returned around the time she must have fallen. Sally tried to make the teacher believe, but the teacher insisted that Henry could not be in two places at once.

The figure's hot breath brought Henry out of his visions as his deep, dark eyes swallowed his remaining reason and left him standing with his mouth agape. The figure looked at him and rumbled, "Baaaaad boy," his thundering voice knocking the breath from the boy's chest. Henry wanted to protest and tried to say anything, but no words came out. He stood there, staring in terror.

Reaching into his sack, the figure pulled out a small orb shaped like a bell and held it before Henry's eyes. A bright golden glow radiated from the orb, intensifying as it seemed to expand and fill the room. Henry was wrapped in its golden brilliance, but he felt icy cold instead of warmth like the color suggested. Awash in the overwhelming glow, his body tingled until it felt like a million ants were crawling across his skin. As the light reached a blinding crescendo, it erased everything in the room until nothing remained but pure, searing light.

Suddenly, the light was gone, along with the figure and Henry, and all that remained was a swirl of snowflakes. Outside, the bells of a sleigh jingled overhead as it raced off towards the nearly full moon while deep chuckles of "Ho! Ho! Ho!" carried on the wind.

The next morning, Jim and Linda made their way down to the living room and settled onto the couch in front of their Christmas tree. With sleep still clouding their eyes, it took them a moment to notice all the gifts beneath the tree. Their cat leaped into Jim's lap just as Linda noticed one package that stood out from the rest. Moving closer, she saw her name on the tag. The gift was wrapped in antique paper, which felt like a blend of linen and silk – special and unique, unlike anything she had seen before. Puzzled, she began to unwrap it.

12

A CHRISTMAS MENAGERIE

As the antique paper peeled away and the lid fell back, a gasp escaped Linda's lips and her hand flew to her mouth. Jim asked what was wrong, and she slowly pulled an antique porcelain figure from the box in response – a ballet dancer posed on the tip of her toe. One arm gracefully arched over her, the fingers touching her head, while the other extended straight from her shoulder, ending in a point. It was the figure her mother had given her before she died, a treasure she had long forgotten. Tears pooled in her eyes as she turned to Jim, cradling the beloved gift. Confused, he asked softly, "Wasn't it lost?"

"I thought it was," she replied in a daze. They pause in silence, staring vacantly at each other as if waiting for something or someone to join them. After a moment, they snapped back to the present, and Jim began handing gifts to Linda to unwrap. They laughed and cried as they opened each gift, the warmth of Christmas Day filling them both. Linda gazed lovingly at Jim before leaning in for a kiss. Smiling, she looked into his eyes and softly said, "Merry Christmas."

II

Christmas Shadows

A CHRISTMAS MENAGERIE

Sarah woke to the sounds of jingling and scraping; something was moving in her room. She slowly opened her eyes to the darkness surrounding her. Outside, the full moon was hidden behind a thick veil of clouds, adding an extra bluish gloom to her room. A quiet dread crept up her spine. She shook herself and muttered that she wasn't scared – that was for babies. The last words she remembered from her father echoed in her mind: no kid of his would be scared or weak. But he wasn't here in this room, wrapped in a darkness that seemed to chill her to the bone.

As Sarah surveyed her surroundings, her eyes drifted to the corner nearest to her closet. That corner seemed darker than anywhere else in her room, almost as if the shadows themselves were alive and breathing. *Are they?* Sarah asked herself. Before the question fully formed in her mind, she heard a slow, deep inhale. Two red slits appeared above the doorframe, slowly widening into fiery orbs. As the menacing eyes locked onto her, Sarah's stomach dropped. She was frozen in place, unable to breathe or think, held captive by primal fear.

At that moment, she realized the shadow was changing, bulging forward like water, forming a droplet. Inch by inch, the darkness swelled and extended. Sarah slid away until her back pressed firmly against the headboard of her small bed. Transfixed with terror, she watched as the shadow took shape, its hand reaching out with four fingers curled back, leaving one sharp talon pointed at her. Her blood turned to ice as a sound echoed deep within her mind: "Saahh-raah."

17

CHRISTMAS SHADOWS

The shadow lurched forward into a small pool of light, revealing its thin hand, the bones and tendons starkly visible. It crept closer until the entire arm emerged, and the rest of the shadow solidified into a massive figure. Sarah craned her neck upward, straining to see where the figure's head might be, but instead found a dark red hood obscuring his face.

The figure's gaze bore into her as he slowly spoke, "Schooose." Sarah blinked in confusion. *Did he just say shoes?* she wondered. As if to answer, the figure slowly repeated, "Schoooose," his tone heavy with annoyance at her lack of understanding. His deep, rumbling voice rippled through her, reminding Sarah of her science teacher's description of an earthquake.

In the blink of an eye, the figure appeared at her bedside, his hand hovering mere inches from her face. She tried to pull back, but her head bumped into the wall behind her. Slowly, his hand opened, revealing all five fingers tipped with dark talons that glinted faintly in the room's dim light. His hand crossed the gap between them and wrapped firmly around her shoulder.

As Sarah felt the firm grasp, her mind reeled in terror. *Is this the end? Will anyone even miss me?* Sadness crept over her as the figure hissed, "Sssssssee." The room plunged into darkness, and Sarah began to fall. Her final thought was, *This is it.*

A CHRISTMAS MENAGERIE

An intense white light blinded Sarah. Instinctively, she raised her hand to block it, but it had no effect. She blinked repeatedly. Somewhere in the distance, she could make out a sound, muffled and low. After a moment, the light dimmed, and the sound gradually became clear. This place seemed oddly familiar to her.

Still blinking rapidly, she began to notice the features of the room. The walls were painted robin's egg blue, adorned by dainty yellow flowers. By the door stood a vanity with an oval mirror, reflecting a gaggle of dolls arranged on the nearby canopied daybed. She stepped towards the window and peered through its sheer lace curtains into the starless night littered with streetlights. "I know this place," she murmured.

By the bed sat an antique rocking chair holding an oversized, fuzzy teddy bear adorned with a red satin bow around its neck. "Charlie!" she squealed, running to him.

As she picked up the bear, a rush of memories flooded her thoughts. Her heart became heavy with emotion, and small tears formed in her eyes. In the back of her mind, she heard a raspy, low growl that seemed to say, "reeee-mem-burrrr." The word lodged itself inside her and sent shivers crawling across her skin. Still reeling from the voice, she lifted her head as the muffled sounds of an argument seeped into the room.

Sarah recognized the voices of her mother and father and strained to make out their words. Moving shakily towards the door, she stepped lightly so as not to be heard. Ever so slowly, she began to turn the shiny brass knob, little by little, until she

19

heard the faint click of the latch retracting. She inhaled sharply and froze, waiting to see if she had been heard. The arguing continued, and her presence remained unnoticed.

The door caught briefly when she pulled on the knob, sticking for a moment before swinging free of the doorjamb. After carefully easing it open the rest of the way, she could hear the fighting in sharp detail. It all came back to her – this argument, this night. Sarah stood there for what felt like an eternity, listening to them sling insults at one another. As the argument escalated, she heard her father yell at her mother that no child of his could ever be weak or scared.

"She has a right to be scared, Thomas," her mother fired back. "She's a child who was just told she might not make it to adulthood."

"Life is hard!" Thomas yelled. "None of us have it easy. The doctors don't know everything, and she needs to toughen up and face reality."

Behind her, Sarah heard sobbing and sniffling. She cautiously turned and looked over her shoulder back into her room. On the bed was a younger version of herself with the covers pulled up around her neck as she held her bear, Charlie, as tightly as she could. Averting her eyes, Sarah realized this was her father's last night in the house. It was the night he left them forever.

She was pulled back into the moment when the front door slammed with such force that it shook the house. At that

20

moment, she again heard the raspy, low growl that seemed to say, "reeee-mem-burrrrr," and darkness descended upon her.

When the darkness lifted, Sarah was greeted by the smell of cleaning supplies – the distinct, sharp odor of disinfectant used to sanitize every possible surface in schools. It was so pervasive that she could not only smell it but also taste it. The bland shade of beige on the walls, ceiling, and floor blended into a seamless vista, making it hard to tell where one ended and the other began. Ahead of her, the hall was flanked by lockers on each side, standing only about three feet high.

Halfway up the hall, a group of children stood in a circle around two others. Voices were raised as some kids chanted, urging someone on, while others jeered at someone lying on the ground.

Sarah stepped towards the crowd, thinking she would never get close enough to see what was happening. As she approached, the crowd seemed to part before her, yet no one turned to acknowledge her presence. When the gap widened, Sarah stepped forward and finally saw what everyone was fixated on. In front of her, a girl loomed over a crying boy on the ground.

"Andy, the pantywaist," the girl taunted loudly. "You're such a baby, pantywaist."

Andy tried to stand up, but the girl standing over him raised her leg and pushed him to the ground with her foot. The crowd laughed and began chanting, "Pantywaist, pantywaist, pantywaist!" The girl turned towards the crowd with a sneer on

CHRISTMAS SHADOWS

her face and a fist in the air, as if she had just conquered the Mongol hordes.

As the girl's face came into view, Sarah instantly recognized it as her own, only two years younger, and she saw that the boy on the ground was Andy Whitehall. Andy, the shyest kid in school, always kept to himself during recess. He was asthmatic and allergic to almost everything. Having transferred to younger Sarah's school that year, he had no friends, making him an easy target. Younger Sarah recognized his timid nature, and it made her angry to think someone could be so weak and scared. The world is hard, and so must you be.

Andy looked up at younger Sarah and breathlessly stammered, "P-p-p-leash," his asthma and stuttering problem contorting the word. She let out a cruel laugh, amused by his pathetic state. Andy braced himself, sliding his elbows under him with his palms flat on the floor. Gradually, he pushed himself to his knees and tried to stand again, but she gave him a rough shove, sending him sprawling backward. He hit his head as he fell, and tears welled in his eyes. "Are you gonna cry?" she taunted, laughing at him.

As Sarah watched in horror, she realized how cruel she had grown since her father walked out. She had taken his parting words to heart, vowing never to show weakness or fear again. Approaching the world with bitterness, she despised weakness in others and asserted dominance over anyone who showed fear. Now, she wanted to push her younger self aside and help Andy. She knew what it felt like to be abandoned and realized she should have been helping him, not hurting him.

A CHRISTMAS MENAGERIE

The tormenting continued, and her stomach twisted with disgust for who she had become. She wanted to run away from the scene, but it felt like a clawed hand was holding her in place.

"Why are you showing me this? Why can't I leave?" she cried.

The figure's only response was a low hiss, "Sssssssee."

Sarah tried to raise her hands to cover her eyes, but they felt like heavy chains were weighing them down. She squeezed her eyes shut and begged for the scene to stop. As she continued to plead, the sounds began to retreat into the distance. The taunting became softer, and the smell of the school faded into a distant memory.

The world seemed to spin faster than usual, leaving Sarah's head throbbing from the sensation. She stretched out her arms to steady herself, but the dizziness persisted. Gradually, the spinning slowed, and colors began to take shape. Behind her, she heard someone stumble into a table, followed by a loud crash of shattering glass, shaking her from her daze.

She turned towards the source of the commotion to find a woman in a stained housecoat and messy hair muttering something Sarah couldn't quite make out. The muttering gave way to a harsh voice that rang through the room. "Where is my damned drink?" the woman snarled. "You little coward, did you take my drink again?"

There was no mistaking the voice – it was her mother, Samantha. This was Christmas Eve last year, just another

CHRISTMAS SHADOWS

chaotic night around their house. Samantha would come home from work, have a drink, then another, and then another. Before dinner was even on the table, she'd already be completely hammered, leaving Sarah to fend for herself.

As Samantha grew drunker, the memories of that argument three years ago came flooding back to her – the final blow in a marriage that had been unraveling ever since Sarah was born and the night John had left her to carry it all herself. No matter how she ended up here, her anger knew no direction, lashing out at the only person within reach.

Standing uncomfortably nearby, Sarah eyed the shards of glass still scattered on the floor near the table her mother had stumbled into earlier. She crouched down to pick them up, jostling the table in the process and sending its remaining contents clattering onto the floor. She paused, her hand hovering over the debris, as her mother's voice cut through the brief silence.

"Will you... will you stop... ruining everything?" Samantha stammered, her slurred words stumbling over each other.

Sarah froze. Did her mother mean the mess or something more? The words stung, leaving her wondering why her mother turned on her after her father left. Did she blame Sarah for her father leaving? Did she think Sarah ruined their family? *Had* she ruined their family?

Samantha tipped the bottle of tequila to her lips and drained the last of its contents. Moments later, the bottle

24

A CHRISTMAS MENAGERIE

slipped from her grasp and rolled lazily across the floor. Seeing her mother passed out on the couch, Sarah couldn't help but feel a pang of sympathy, wanting nothing more than to help her mother feel better.

She carried the empty bottle to the kitchen, then collected the rest – in various stages of emptiness – and poured their contents down the drain. Erasing the last traces, she took the empty bottles down the hall to the trash chute, dropping them in one by one. She slipped back inside, crept to her room, and crawled into bed.

There would be no Christmas again this year since her mother had spent all their money feeding her drinking problem. Still, Sarah clung to hope, silently praying for Santa to bring her just one gift – the gift of her mother's love instead of hate. As tears filled young Sarah's eyes, she drifted off to sleep.

As Sarah's eyes adjusted to the darkness, she realized she was back in her room. Turning her head, she saw the figure who had set everything in motion that night, his face still hidden beneath a deep red hood trimmed in white fur. Two red-orange eyes, glowing like coals, peered out at her as his hot breath washed over her face, causing her eyes to sting. She opened her mouth to scream, but no sound came out. A tongue flicked out of the figure's mouth, gliding across his lips before darting back

CHRISTMAS SHADOWS

into his mouth. He drew a long, slow breath and repeated, "Sssch-ooooose."

Sarah reeled from everything she had just witnessed. She could see the darkness she had descended into and how her mother was slipping further away. Tears flowed down her cheeks as she hungrily gulped air, her trembling breaths unsteady. The figure's voice echoed within her, and suddenly, she understood – it was saying *choose*. Finding her voice again, she timidly asked, "Choose what?"

Without answering, the figure reached out with one long, clawed finger and firmly tapped her chest directly above her racing heart. Still confused, she felt a wave of dread sweep over her. What choice was he asking her to make? The memories she had just relived swirled in her mind as her thoughts gravitated to her mother – how unhappy she had become and how little Sarah had been able to help. Perhaps her father had been right to think she wasn't strong enough.

In this moment of despair, Sarah realized how much her pain had shaped her. Her loss, her anger, her guilt – it had all come out as cruelty towards others. This was never the choice she wanted.

Amidst the pain, warm memories surfaced: the careful thought her mother put into Christmas gifts, the times they went for walks in the park or shopping for a new dress, and the birthday parties her mother tirelessly prepared for her. Her sadness turned to longing as she started sobbing uncontrollably.

26

A CHRISTMAS MENAGERIE

"I just want our life back," she sobbed. "I want us to be happy again."

In response, the figure slowly raised an arm, his clawed fingers closed into a fist. Sarah's chest tightened as his hand opened to reveal an old iron bell resting in his palm. A faint golden glow began to seep from the bell, pulsing softly at first but growing stronger each moment. The light expanded, spilling across the room and chasing shadows to the corners, until its intensity forced Sarah to look away. Her heart pounded in her chest – this was it. Whatever was going to happen to her would happen now.

As Sarah sat crying heavily, the figure began to shift and change. The dark tinges of his outfit became bright and crisp, and his claws withdrew, softening into green-mittened hands. A flowing white beard cascaded from beneath the hood, and the glowing red-orange eyes became sparkling blue. All Sarah heard before the room went black was a deep, festive "Ho! Ho! Ho!"

For a moment, there was nothing – no sound, no sight, only an overwhelming stillness. Then, as if no time had passed, Sarah found herself in a room bathed in warm light from a nearby window. She looked around, somehow surprised to find herself in her own bed. Glancing out the window, she noticed a fresh blanket of snow covering the ground. Her eyes were swollen, hinting at a night of crying, although she struggled to recall what had caused it. A lingering sense of sadness tugged at her, but when she tried to remember why, it slipped away like a puddle drying in the sun.

27

CHRISTMAS SHADOWS

She swung her legs over the edge of the bed, suddenly remembering it was Christmas morning. Jumping to her feet, she grabbed Charlie and hurried to the living room, where their meager Christmas tree stood with a couple of small gifts that Sarah had scrounged up to buy. Her mother lay asleep on the couch, just as she had the night before. Sarah cautiously stepped towards her, remembering that she had been drinking.

Bending close to her mother's ear, she gently shook her shoulder and whispered, "Merry Christmas, Mom. I love you." For a moment, nothing happened. Then, as if touched by some Christmas magic, her mother stirred. Sarah reflexively pulled back, half expecting her mother to start yelling. Instead, her mother stretched and yawned, looking at her with quiet confusion as Sarah offered to make breakfast.

After preparing the meal, she returned with a mug of coffee and a plate of food for her mother. Sarah looked at her solemnly as she ate, hesitating before saying, "I'm sorry Dad left because of me. You deserve to be happy." Her mother froze mid-bite, the fork slipping from her hand and landing in her lap. Shock spread across her face as tears filled her eyes.

"Oh honey," her mother said, her voice trembling, "your dad didn't leave because of you. Where did you hear that?" Sarah recounted the night she heard them arguing while Samantha stared in disbelief, the last few years becoming clearer. Her daughter's actions and words now made more sense — she had been blaming herself, acting out of guilt in addition to her pain and loss. Not knowing what else to say, Samantha reached for her daughter and pulled her in for a tight

A CHRISTMAS MENAGERIE

hug. "I love you, Sarah," she said softly. Sarah felt as if a weight had been lifted off her shoulders and that things might finally have a chance to get better.

Across the room, a northern window offered a clear view of the wooded lot in the backyard – and a clear view of the living room from the wooded lot. Outside, unnoticed amongst the shadows, a figure peered through the window. Draped in a long red robe trimmed in white fur, his face was framed by a fluffy white beard and partially hidden by a fur-trimmed red hood. As he gazed into their home at the touching moment within, his eyes twinkled with approval, and he slowly uttered, "Mare-eeee Chrisssss-masss!"

He Knows If You've Been Bad or Good

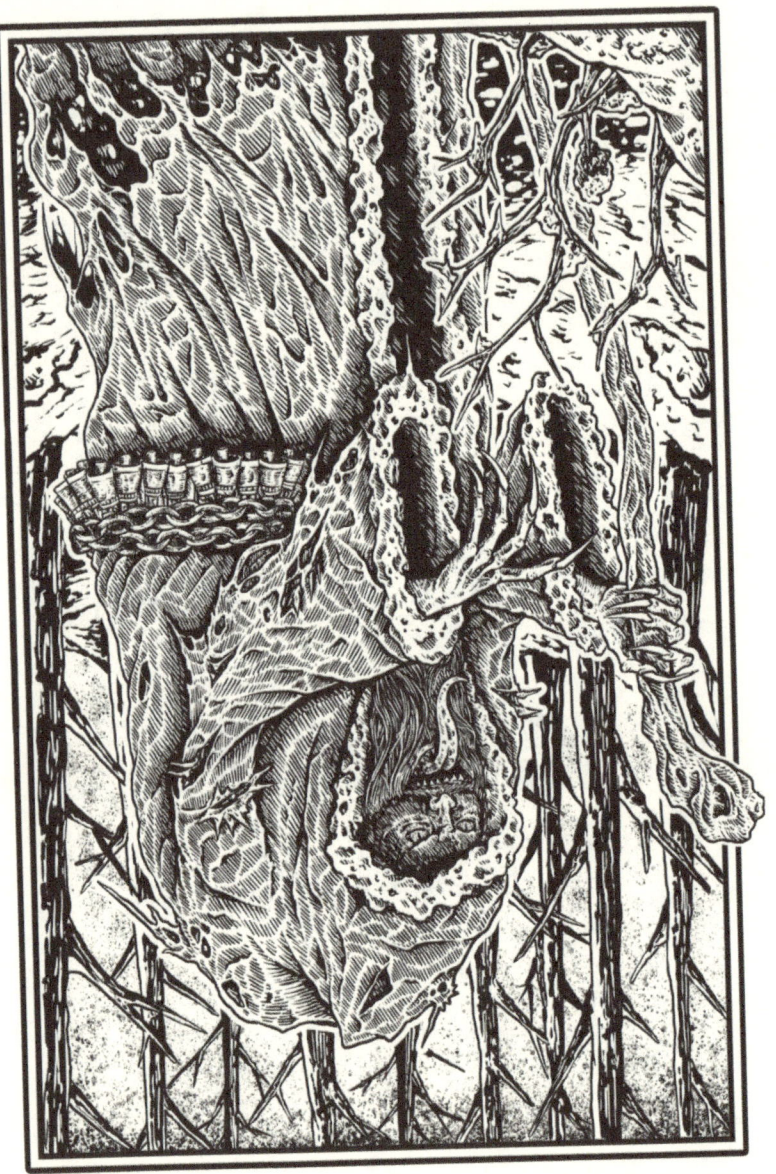

A CHRISTMAS MENAGERIE

Kristoff was a small kid, even by kid standards. As such, he passed most people by without them affording him a second glance. He had grown somewhat used to it during his time living on his own. At six years of age, he had seen a great many of the world's atrocities, but it always amazed him how children on the street were treated, especially by adults who had children of their own. After all, this was the time of year when Santa Claus watched everyone with intent eyes, deciding who was bad and who was good.

Kristoff didn't have much other than the clothes on his back. He had a small-brimmed hat that was his father's; pants, a shirt, and a threadbare overcoat given to him by a monk from the local church; and a pair of shoes with more holes than leather. Still, it was better than what many had living on the streets, that's for sure. Kristoff knew the world was hard, but he also knew you had to keep going.

Today was Christmas Eve, a day of magic and wonder for most. The sun crept across the alleyway and shone into Kristoff's eyes, pulling him from his slumber. His stomach grumbled as if to say, "Good morning." He wasn't sure when he last ate, but judging by the sound, it had been a while. Stretching his legs, he moved around a bit before heading out of the alley and into the city's streets.

While growing up on the streets was hard, it had moments of beauty and wonder, and this day was one of them. A blanket of snow covered the otherwise dirty streets. People were too caught up in their shopping and bustling around to notice, but Kristoff took each detail into memory as if it were the last time

HE KNOWS IF YOU'VE BEEN BAD OR GOOD

he would see it. The way the snow clung to the roof just over the windows reminded him of the bushy eyebrows of the monk who gave him his clothes. The way the sun played across the frozen surface of the snow reminded him of the twinkling stars at night. To him, it was a wondrous beauty that only appeared for a brief time.

As he made his way through the streets, most people ignored him and bumped him out of the way. Some looked at him with disgust, their eyes catching on the lines of dirt streaking his face and his tattered clothing. Others clutched their purses tightly, thinking he was a pickpocket trying to steal their possessions. None of this mattered to Kristoff; he was on a mission. That mission was to head just outside the city to a small farm with a stand of fruit trees – a place he often visited when hungry. This time of year, he could still find an apple or two that had not been devoured by woodland animals or picked for sale by the farmer. Sometimes – just sometimes, mind you – the farmer's wife would see him and, out of pity, offer him something to eat before tossing it to the hogs.

It was almost mid-afternoon when he reached the little farm outside the city. He searched the trees and the ground beneath for some time before finding an apple that still had some good parts on it and placing it in his small sack. As he was leaving the field, the farmer yelled in his direction, and Kristoff froze in his tracks. He turned towards the sound and saw the farmer walking towards him. Out of fear, he slowly started to back away, but the farmer yelled at him to stop.

A CHRISTMAS MENAGERIE

Panicked, he froze in place again. The farmer made his way to Kristoff and eyed him up and down.

"Good afternoon, young master," the farmer said, tipping his hat.

Kristoff swallowed hard and stammered, "Good afternoon, sir."

"The harvest was light this year, so I'm surprised you found anything left," the farmer remarked. Knowing he had been caught, Kristoff reached into his bag and pulled out the cast-off, misshapen apple he had found. "Just this," he confessed timidly.

Seeing the apple, the farmer's heart sank, feeling even more pity for Kristoff than he and his wife already did. They also knew the hardships this time of year could bring and what it was like to have little in the way of wealth. "Here you are," the farmer offered, extending his arms to Kristoff. "Take this. It's the best I can do."

To Kristoff's shock, it was a small loaf of bread and some remnants of cheese. He hesitated before reaching out and accepting them, placing each piece delicately in his sack. Tears filled his eyes as he seldom saw this kind of kindness. "Thank you, sir," he uttered shyly.

"It's not much," the farmer continued, "but it's from our farm and more than we need, and you seem hungry." With that, he wished Kristoff well and returned to his small cottage. Kristoff stood there for a few moments longer, overwhelmed

35

HE KNOWS IF YOU'VE BEEN BAD OR GOOD

with gratitude. Letting out a breath he hadn't realized he was holding, he turned and started his journey back to the city.

After walking for what felt like miles, Kristoff realized he wouldn't make it back by nightfall. He spotted a fire glowing in a nearby glen, its flickering light beckoning from afar, so he changed course and cautiously approached it. The closer he got, the more he longed to be near its red-orange flames and feel the soft touches of warmth cascade over him, chasing away the night's chill.

Sitting by the fire was a gaunt, grey-haired man, his clothes nearly as threadbare as Kristoff's. Just outside the ring of firelight, Kristoff stopped and timidly called, "Hello?"

"Hello there," the stranger echoed, slowly lifting his gaze from the fire. "Aren't you a bit young to be out on a night like this? You look frozen."

Kristoff scrutinized the ragged character, unsure what to make of him, but the warmth of the fire proved irresistible. "Yes, sir, I am," he hesitantly admitted. "May I please sit by your fire?"

The man chuckled softly. "It's all I have," he said, "but you're welcome to it."

Kristoff slowly moved towards the fire, staying close to the trees in case he needed to make an early exit. Looking around, he noticed that the man had nothing but the fire to keep him warm – no blanket to sleep under, no pillow to rest his head on, and no shelter from the elements. The only other thing Kristoff saw was a steaming kettle hanging over the fire.

36

A CHRISTMAS MENAGERIE

"You look hungry," the man observed. "I'm sorry I don't have anything to offer you."

Kristoff said it was okay as his thoughts turned to the bread, cheese, and moldered apple in his bag. "You look hungry too," he noted, studying him by the firelight.

The man sighed heavily and replied that he hadn't eaten in almost a week. "I've asked people for help, but they just ignore me," he explained. "I tried hunting, but I'm too weak to do much of anything now."

Kristoff felt a pang of sympathy as he looked at his sack. Reaching inside, he pulled out the bread and cheese and offered them to his host.

"I can't take that," the man objected, shaking his head. "You need it as much as I do."

Kristoff pushed the food closer. "It's okay, mister," he insisted, "I have more. Please take it."

The haggard man hesitated, then accepted his offer with a grateful smile and began eating. Meanwhile, Kristoff pulled out the apple, carefully ate around the bad spots, and threw the remains into the woods for the animals to finish.

The fire was soothing, and soon Kristoff felt his eyes grow heavy until the darkness of sleep overtook him. After a while, he was jolted awake by a sound he couldn't quite place. Thinking it might have been a dream, he tried to go back to sleep.

37

HE KNOWS IF YOU'VE BEEN BAD OR GOOD

There it was again – a tinkling sound, like bells, and footsteps crunching in the snow. At first, Kristoff thought it was his new companion, but the man was fast asleep on the other side of the fire. The sounds grew louder, and Kristoff couldn't help but wonder what – or who – was making them.

He rose and started towards the noise, pausing whenever the sounds stopped and continuing when they resumed so that he could stay on the right path. A short distance later, he came upon a small clearing where the noise seemed to originate. Slowly, he crept forward, straining to hear anything that might warn him to turn back.

The tinkling now carried a clanking sound, much louder than before. In front of Kristoff stood a massive oak tree – so large that he would need three more of himself to wrap around it. Placing his hands firmly on the rough bark, he listened again, then cautiously peered around the trunk.

What he saw stopped him in his tracks.

In the clearing ahead stood a formidable figure, hunched slightly at the shoulders and draped in a tattered robe trimmed in what must have once been white rabbit fur. Now, the colors were muted, and the fur was darkened with age and dirt, though it still looked quite warm. Around the figure's waist hung heavy chains with thick links, each attached to a bell by a ring, allowing them to slide and clink against one another.

Kristoff crept around the tree to get a better view. As he moved, his coat snagged on the rough bark, creating a crunching sound as it broke free. The noise seemed unnaturally

38

A CHRISTMAS MENAGERIE

loud in the stillness, and Kristoff froze, his heart pounding in his ears. Ahead, the figure shifted and began to turn towards him, the faint tinkling of bells mingling with the clank of chains. Kristoff's breath caught as he realized the figure had heard him, and now, as he began to turn, the details of his towering form became clearer.

The figure was broad-chested and taller than an average man, with a sack slung over his shoulder, stuffed to the point of bursting. One massive hand curled around a staff of some kind, his fingers ending in sharp claws or talons. As his gaze traveled up the figure's arm, Kristoff realized he was looking directly at him from beneath a hood that cast a black shadow where its face should be. All Kristoff could see under the hood were two glowing red-orange eyes, a flowing white beard, and a long tongue flicking around as if tasting the air.

Before Kristoff could think, his feet carried him out from behind the tree towards the imposing figure. As he stepped closer, he heard himself whisper, "Santa?" In his mind, he knew this monstrous figure couldn't possibly be Santa, but somehow, deep inside, he felt it *had* to be.

The figure approached Kristoff as well, his arm outstretched, shifting the staff forward with each deliberate step. As they closed the distance, the figure lowered his sack and extended a hand towards Kristoff, who instinctively returned the gesture. The moment his small hand touched the outstretched claw, a blindingly bright light erupted, and the world slowly dissolved around them.

HE KNOWS IF YOU'VE BEEN BAD OR GOOD

Kristoff blinked several times, trying to regain his vision. The intense light gradually faded, leaving behind vague outlines that slowly solidified. When his sight finally returned, he found himself standing in a room filled with beds, each occupied by a person. Sounds began to filter in as well – coughing, wailing, and a pervasive sadness that hung in the air.

Ahead, in a dimly lit corner of the room, he noticed two beds pushed closer together than the rest – one with a man and the other with a woman. At the foot of her bed lay a small child-shaped lump, no older than three years. The figure nudged Kristoff forward, urging him to move closer. One hesitant step, then another, and soon he was close enough to make out the features of the people in the beds.

"Momma, Poppa?" he gasped. "Is that you?"

They continued as they were, never looking in his direction. Kristoff spoke again, a little louder this time, but still got no response. He turned to the figure to ask if they could hear him, but the figure only stared ahead, as if curious about what would happen next.

The woman leaned forward and stroked the sleeping boy's head. Feeling his mother's touch, the child looked up and smiled. He inched towards her, seeing the worry and fear in her eyes but pretending not to notice. Once close enough, she wrapped him in her arms and hugged him tightly.

A CHRISTMAS MENAGERIE

The boy's father called to him next, and he leaped from one parent's bed to the other. "Merry Christmas, Kristoff," the man sighed, patting his son on the head. "Sorry that we can't be at home this year."

"It's okay, Poppa," the young boy replied. "I still have you and Momma."

The man tried to muster a reassuring expression for his son as he looked deep into his eyes. "You're growing up so quickly," he declared. "I'm so proud of you. You'll grow up to be a fine man one day. You will help people and be kind – I'm sure of it."

"Yes, Poppa," the boy said, smiling naively. "I'll be just like you and Momma."

"No," his father replied sullenly. "You'll be better than us. You will do great things… I only wish we could be there to see it happen."

The boy didn't fully understand his father's words, so he simply smiled in return. "You will, Poppa," he assured him with a wink. "You will."

Teary-eyed, Kristoff turned towards the figure. "This was the last time I ever saw my momma and poppa," he lamented. "They went away and left me here to wait for them."

With that, another blindingly bright light filled the space around them. Kristoff pleaded, "Wait! I want to see them. I want to tell them goodbye – and that I love them. I never got to tell them." But it was too late.

41

HE KNOWS IF YOU'VE BEEN BAD OR GOOD

As the bright light faded, Kristoff and the figure stood before a monastery adorned with magnificent stained-glass windows. To the right of the building, a stone wall concealed a small garden and courtyard. "I know this place!" Kristoff exclaimed. In an instant, he darted forward to slip through a broken section of the wall. As he squeezed through the crack, he realized the figure was already inside, waiting for him.

Ahead, the courtyard was filled with a large group of children, all orphaned in some way – all of whom he recognized. Two monks stood nearby, speaking in hushed tones about how they couldn't possibly clothe and feed all these boys. Their conversation was heavy with despair, laden with remarks about godless times and the rising number of children left parentless by the plague. All hope seemed to be lost. The monks, however, failed to notice that young Kristoff had been playing in the bushes nearby and had overheard every word.

Kristoff had been playing with Timothy, the newest addition to the monastery. Timothy's family had also fallen victim to the sickness, leaving him utterly alone, and Kristoff had been doing his best to help the newcomer fit in. Now, after hearing the monks' grim words, Kristoff couldn't help but worry about what would become of Timothy and the other children.

As dinnertime approached, Kristoff helped Timothy to the dining hall, where tonight's meal seemed much smaller than usual. The abbot stood at the head of the hall, called for everyone's attention, and explained that times were getting hard, and even God's children must sometimes tighten their

42

A CHRISTMAS MENAGERIE

belts. Young Kristoff was old enough to understand this meant food was becoming scarce.

Looking down at the bread and soup in front of him, he decided that Timothy needed it more than he did. Quietly, he spooned some of his soup into Timothy's bowl whenever he wasn't looking. After the third time, Timothy looked at him and asked, "Aren't you gonna eat?"

Kristoff replied that he'd had a big lunch and wasn't really hungry, urging Timothy to go ahead and finish his food. Timothy smiled and eagerly devoured the meal in front of him.

After dinner, with his belly full, Timothy followed Kristoff to their beds, chattering excitedly about what they might do tomorrow. As they passed the monks' quarters, Kristoff overheard someone say there were more children than beds and that the monastery could no longer support them all.

When they reached the dormitory, Kristoff helped Timothy into bed and began telling him the story of Santa Claus as his friend drifted off to sleep. Looking down at him, Kristoff felt a deep ache in his chest, knowing there was a chance that Timothy might be sent away. This was his first real friend.

Kristoff had been at the monastery for two years, and he knew he was the oldest one there. Rising slowly from Timothy's bedside, he decided he would leave the monastery so Timothy wouldn't have to. He reached under his bed and retrieved the few small toys and belongings he owned. Gently, he placed

HE KNOWS IF YOU'VE BEEN BAD OR GOOD

them in Timothy's socks, which were hanging at the end of his bed, knowing his friend would find them in the morning.

With that, Kristoff packed up what few clothes he had, along with a blanket and pillow, and crept towards the window in the back corner of the room. Quietly, he slid it open, slipped through the narrow gap, and pulled it shut behind him. Moving quickly, he made his way to the crack in the garden wall and disappeared into the night.

Young Kristoff failed to notice the abbot watching him leave from his window. Leaving his quarters, the abbot made his way to Kristoff's bed, where he found a note detailing all that Kristoff had overheard and why he was leaving. The last line begged the abbot to keep Timothy safe and warm inside the monastery for as long as he could.

As the older Kristoff stood in the figure's shadow, watching the abbot read his note, a tear slipped down his cheek.

The world dissolved into a bright light again as the scene fell away.

Two more times this happened, each memory showing that Kristoff understood how dark the world could be, yet he kept going. Whenever he encountered someone in greater need than himself, he gave what little he had, recalling his father's words and how helping others embodied the spirit of Christmas. That was his guiding star, the light that kept him from being swallowed by the massive world and all its hardships. He held onto the belief that he could make a

44

A CHRISTMAS MENAGERIE

difference, somehow – a difference like his parents made to him.

As Kristoff blinked repeatedly, he realized he and the figure were back in the glen where they had started. But as he looked up, the figure appeared different from a moment ago. The moonlight illuminated a vibrant red robe trimmed with the whitest rabbit fur Kristoff had ever seen, paired with dark green pants that reminded him of the stories he'd heard about Laplanders. The hood of his robe was pushed back just enough to reveal a joyous round face with bright blue eyes, bushy white eyebrows, and a long flowing beard as white as new-fallen snow. Kristoff's eyes widened in astonishment as the figure turned towards him. He opened his mouth to speak, but his voice cracked as he tried to say the name.

Raising a hand and resting it on Kristoff's small shoulder, the figure cocked his head to one side and rumbled, "Ho! Ho! Ho! Mare-eeee Chrisssss-masss!" before gesturing towards the clearing ahead. Kristoff's eyes followed the gesture to a sleigh pulled by eight reindeer. Overflowing with excitement – a feeling he hadn't experienced many times before – he looked up at the figure and questioned, "Are you asking me to come with you?" The figure nodded and pointed towards the sleigh once more.

45

HE KNOWS IF YOU'VE BEEN BAD OR GOOD

Without a moment's hesitation, Kristoff dashed towards the sleigh. After all, who could pass up a ride with Santa on this of all nights? The figure mounted the sleigh beside Kristoff, gently took up the reins, and gave them a single snap. The reindeer instantly sprang to life. The sleigh caught for the briefest of moments before the snow surrendered its grasp on the runners, allowing them to glide forward. Within about ten feet, the sleigh began to climb into the air.

A few moments later, Kristoff realized they were soaring above the treetops. The moon seemed so close that he could reach out and pluck it from the sky. Looking over his shoulder, Kristoff spotted two sacks in the back – one brimming with brightly colored presents and the other bulging with odd shapes and sticks poking out from the top. "One for the good boys and girls and one for the bad ones, right?" Kristoff asked. The figure nodded in agreement.

Kristoff leaned back and took in the wonder of the ride, marveling that no one would ever believe he had soared the night sky with Santa. He tried to memorize every detail as Santa finished his last rounds in the area. Fearing his most wonderful night was coming to an end, he readied himself for the landing that never came. Confused, he glanced at the figure, who only stared straight ahead. Deciding not to dwell on it, Kristoff resolved to simply enjoy the moment.

Suddenly, he spotted a massive building in the distance, speckled with countless glowing lights. He had never seen such a sight. As they drew closer, the structure reminded him of the stories he had heard about the castles in neighboring countries.

A CHRISTMAS MENAGERIE

He stared in wonderment, noticing there was no town nearby. In fact, he hadn't seen anything like a town for a long time.

Sensing Kristoff's confusion, the figure raised an arm and pointed towards the building in the distance. "Hhhhh-ome," he muttered. It took Kristoff a few moments to process the word and understand – this must be the North Pole. He didn't know how to feel, but a mixture of excitement and nervousness filled him almost to the point of bursting.

Once they landed, Kristoff noticed that none of the people who came out to greet the figure seemed especially surprised to see a young boy with him. One of them stepped forward towards the sleigh, where Kristoff still looked quite perplexed. "Welcome, Kristoff Kringle," he announced. "We have great things planned for you."

Kristoff had no words to describe his feelings, having never known such happiness. His only wish was that his momma and poppa could be there with him. The figure gently placed his arm around Kristoff and ushered him through the crowd of helpers. One thought filled Kristoff's mind as he entered the grand castle: *This is going to be amazing.*

IV

The Last Journey

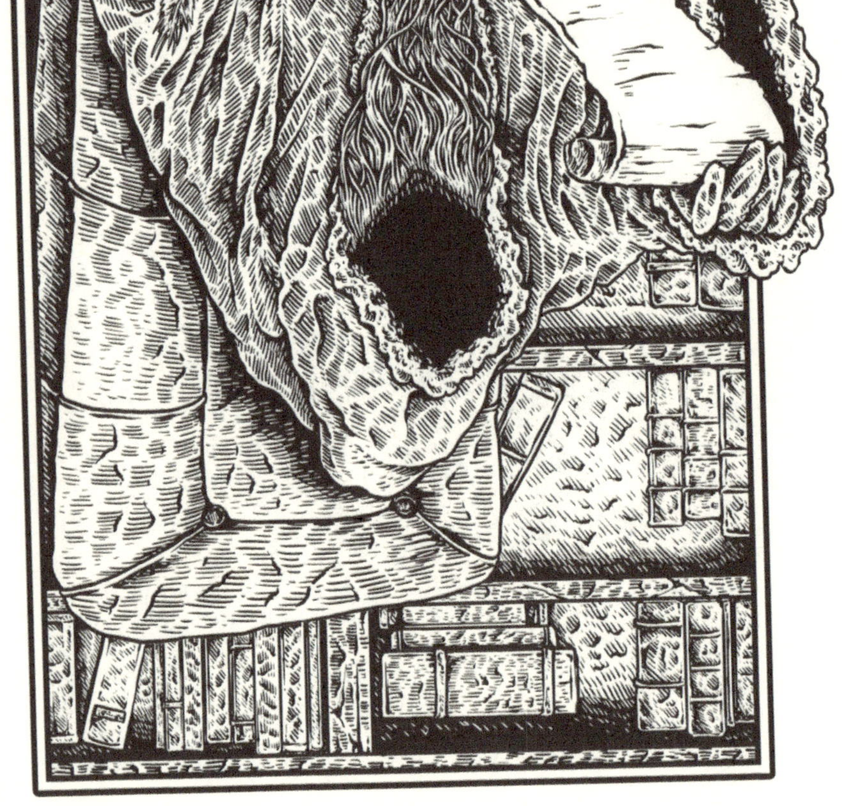

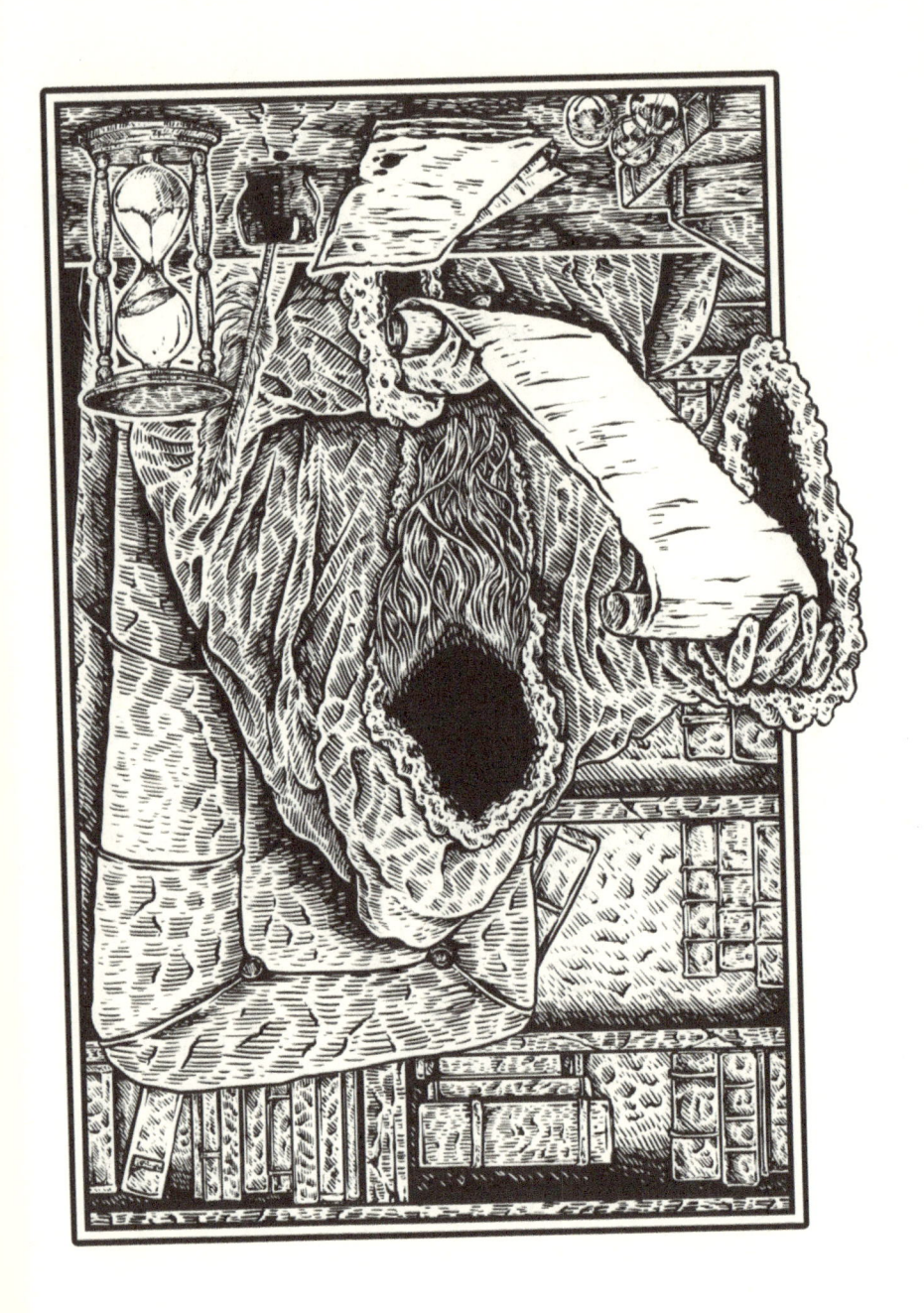

T he air was crisp and refreshing, taking the edge off a long night. The sleigh glided through the sky, pulled by eight reindeer, with the figure at the reins. Weariness seeped into his tired bones, and he was ready for the night to be over.

Below him, the ground was a constant blur of changing scenery. Low, flat plains gave way to hill-studded expanses with a light coating of freshly fallen snow, then onward to deep snow-encrusted mountains. The moon descended below the horizon just as the first touches of morning light crept into sight.

The sleigh only carried the figure, an empty red sack folded neatly on the seat beside him, and a full, velvety, antique black sack resting in the back. With a gentle tug on the right-handed rein, the figure guided his team to turn and begin their descent towards home. The reindeer tossed their heads as they passed through a thick bank of clouds. Beyond the mist stood the peaks of Korvatunturi, where, firmly tucked away from prying eyes, a cluster of buildings encircled a large castle-looking workshop. As the sleigh descended further, a smile tugged at the corner of his mouth, a sparkle returned to his eyes, and a deep, rolling "Hooo! Hooo! Hoo!" escaped his parted lips.

The sleigh streaked across the tops of a dense pine forest that separated Korvatunturi from the town of Savukoski. With its towering trees and shadowed undergrowth, the forest was foreboding enough to keep most people away except for the occasional hunter. The path that winded through it was marked by countless switchbacks and offshoots, ensuring that most wanderers would lose their way.

THE LAST JOURNEY

As he flew over the final stretch of forest, a large frozen lake came into view – the last geographical barrier between the outside world and his domain. At that moment, a herd of reindeer was crossing from one side to the other, briefly catching his eye as the sleigh crossed the remaining distance to his workshop. One final pull of the reins aligned the sleigh with a patch of clear ground and a wooden landing strip. The reindeer slowed as they negotiated the final approach. A few moments later, they came to a peaceful rest before the stable, bustling with activity as excited sounds escaped into the night.

Placing the reins neatly across the front of the sleigh, the figure jumped down as his robe billowed onto the ground. With a sweeping motion, he turned towards the back of the sleigh to retrieve the velvety black sack. As he faced the castle doors, a pair of helpers arrived to assist him. One collected the empty red sack and carried it to a small workshop door while the other began unhooking the reindeer from the sleigh.

With a groan, the figure slung the black sack over his shoulder and moved towards the grand double doors. Leaning his free hand against the heavy oak, he let out a slight grunt and gave a firm push until the doors gave way to the hallway beyond. With a wide step and a slide of his dragging foot, he made his way inside the castle.

Deep within lay a room built ages before the castle that now surrounded it. A narrow door, smoothed by generations of touch, concealed an opening that descended into the mountain, leading to a three-sided chamber with a massive fireplace. The walls were lined with shelves towering fifty feet

A CHRISTMAS MENAGERIE

high, mirrored by rows of equally tall shelves stretching a hundred yards across the floor. At the center stood a time-worn desk fashioned from redwood, its surface strewn with papers, ink bottles, and quills. A few candles flickered faintly, providing barely enough light to read and write by. Tonight, the desk sat empty, waiting for someone to return.

In the distance, approaching footsteps echoed through the halls... a dull step followed by a dragging sound and a faint jingling. Step... drag... jingle...step... drag... jingle. The sounds paused outside of the sturdy old door guarding the room. The latch clicked into motion, and the door creaked open just enough for the figure to step through, the antique black bag still slung across his shoulder.

As he approached the desk, the figure dropped his bag and fell into the chair, letting out a deep sigh that rumbled like distant thunder. His limbs hung heavy with fatigue, but his job was not finished for the night.

On one side of the desk was a large book stand holding an ancient volume, its cover fashioned from animal skin even older than the figure seated at the desk. On the front of the book, in red glowing letters, were the words *"Bad Boys and Girls."* This thick, leather-bound book contained the names of all the bad children – and those on the verge of being bad – from ages past to present. The figure noted grimly that the number of bad children seemed to grow larger with each passing year, and he couldn't help but wonder, *Will there be enough room?*

53

THE LAST JOURNEY

The figure pulled a list from a pouch on his belt and carefully unrolled it. At the top of that list was the year, followed by a series of categories. He meticulously reviewed the list and compared it to the book, scrutinizing the names and checking them off one by one. Once the task was complete, he rolled up the list and placed it on the desk to be filed later.

Rising from the chair, the figure bent over to grab the velvety black sack beside the desk and walked towards the shelves. He turned to the side of the room labeled *"Bad Boys and Girls"* and headed to a section marked by a gold plaque bearing the current year.

The figure untied the sack and reached inside, his fingers closing around a cold iron bell. Pulling it out, he turned it over in his hand to inspect the name deeply etched into its surface. As he held the bell, it began to emit a bright yellow-white light, and his mind was instantly filled with the thoughts of a young child from earlier that night. A deep murmur of satisfaction escaped his throat as he filed the first bell away on a shelf. One by one, he drew the bells from the sack, each one a window into the child he had visited and collected, leaving their parents with no memory of them.

After placing each new bell on its shelf, the figure slowly walked the aisles, noting all he had encountered over the years. Each bell contained a bad child, frozen at the exact age when they met the figure, unaware of how much time had passed them by.

54

A CHRISTMAS MENAGERIE

Next, the figure made his way to the section labeled *"Watch List."* Again, he reached into his antique sack, this time pulling out a snow globe. Globe after globe was pulled from the sack and placed on a shelf, each one containing a detailed replica of a child's home he had visited. His hand encircled the last globe in the bag, pulling it out into the light. As his gaze fell upon it, his mind flashed to the living room of a boy and his parents. In the vision, the boy embraced his mother in a hug so full of emotion that it surprised them both. This brought a smile to the figure's face and gave him hope that the boy had turned a corner.

After delicately placing the remaining globe in its spot, he strode across the room. Rows of shelves labeled *"Good Girls and Boys"* held each year's book, listing all of the good little girls and boys, including an open space for this year's book. He placed the new book in its slot and returned to the desk.

As the figure slumped into the chair, the entirety of the night washed over him. Looking up, he extended his weary arm towards a hand-blown hourglass in one corner of the immense old wooden desk. His fingers wrapped around it, lifting it delicately to inspect the intricate decorations depicting scenes of the surrounding area. As he gazed upon the hourglass, it was clear that time was running out. "Rrr-eeeeest," was all that escaped his mouth.

Suddenly, a knock echoed through the chamber. The narrow door inched open, and a small towheaded boy peeked around the corner, slowly scanning the room. Though he appeared young, he had been a resident of the castle for nearly

THE LAST JOURNEY

three hundred years after being saved one fateful night by the figure. Since then, the figure had taken him under his wing and shown him the magic of the "North Pole."

Although it was located in Korvatunturi, the North Pole wasn't exactly a place. The actual North Pole was an ancient object, its origins lost to the ages. With its power, a person could embody the visage of what would become known throughout history as Santa Claus, Father Christmas, or the host of other names tied to Christmas. That same power shrouded the valley and castle with an image of snow and ice, ensuring that no one would accidentally wander into this most ancient place.

The figure looked up from the desk and quietly beckoned, "Krisss-toff." Hearing his name, Kristoff smiled and ran into the room to give the figure a warm hug. Fatigue and soreness faded slightly as the figure smiled at the boy's embrace. His face softened, and his voice lightened as he addressed him. "My time is almost over, Kristoff," he said gently.

Kristoff blinked; his face contorted in bewilderment. "But… you're Santa," he protested, his voice rising slightly. "You can't quit. The world needs you."

The figure's mind raced at these words. The world did indeed need Santa — more than it realized. Santa was a balancing force. The duty of this position was to keep good and bad in check, to ensure that the scales did not tip too far one way or another, and to preserve the balance that allowed the world to continue functioning as it always had.

56

A CHRISTMAS MENAGERIE

"Not *the* Santa, but *a* Santa," replied the figure, his voice weathered by centuries of weariness. He allowed the words to settle in the silence.

Kristoff's mind spun with the thought of the Santa he knew, not being *the* Santa. Seeing the confusion in Kristoff's eyes, the figure raised a hand to calm him and elaborated, "The role of Santa has been around since the world started. This person is responsible for keeping the balance of good and evil – for making sure that evil doesn't consume the hearts of humanity."

Kristoff listened intently and asked, "So why not remove *all* the evil from the world so that no one has to worry anymore?"

"You cannot force or breed goodness in people," the figure explained. "It has to be chosen. Removing good or evil would force a reset of the world, and all people would perish so the balance could be restored. A forest can only grow so densely before the litter dries out and catches fire. The resulting fire restores nature's balance, allowing new growth to flourish."

The figure rose from the desk and motioned for Kristoff to follow him to the back wall of the cavernous room. They stopped where two paths converged, each flanked by tall shelves. One path had a sign that read *"Bad Boys and Girls,"* while the other's sign read *"Watch List."* The figure turned to face the opposite wall, where a sign read *"Good Girls and Boys."*

Looking down at Kristoff, he continued, "This is our job. We listen to the children and know their deepest and darkest

THE LAST JOURNEY

feelings and fears. If a child strays down the path of being bad
– *very* bad – we judge them accordingly and bring them here."
He pointed to the rows of shelves in the *"Bad Boys and Girls"*
section and added, "We keep them here to prevent them from
inflicting the darkness they have chosen. Those who have yet
to make their choice are shown a better path and placed in the
"Watch List" area. They remain free from these shelves as long
as they make the right choices."

They made their way down the path between the *"Bad Boys
and Girls"* and *"Watch List"* sections, arriving at an ancient
stone door that appeared to have grown from the rock around
it rather than being carved by hand. The figure pushed the door
open and ushered Kristoff inside for the first time.

The room was dark except for a shaft of light that
illuminated a stone pillar in the center. As Kristoff's eyes
adjusted, he saw that, like the previous room, this one was lined
with shelves; however, only one section was filled. Its shelves
held rows of small statues, each carved with such precision that
they almost looked alive, as if ready to leap off the shelf.

"Each one is a previous incarnation of the Spirit of this
time of year," the figure explained. "Each one created a version
that was all their own while preserving parts of the original
Spirit. We are the mirror of what lies in each and every child.
The Spirit a child sees is a reflection of the darkness or light
they carry. That is why you have only ever seen me as Santa."

Kristoff furrowed his brow. "But you are also what they
fear and what they are capable of?" he asked.

58

A CHRISTMAS MENAGERIE

The figure nodded. "Yes, in part, but also so much more. Some children are not surprised by what lies beneath their exterior, so we must magnify that and become stronger. This is how we save those on the verge of making the wrong choice." Guiding Kristoff away from the shelves, he turned to the center of the room.

Before them stood the stone pillar, circled in bright light streaming from a hole in the ceiling. With it, the light carried whispers – whispers of children. Some spoke of what they wished Santa would bring them for Christmas, while others spoke of the dark things they were thinking or doing. Overwhelmed by the sound, Kristoff raised his hands to cover his ears.

The figure looked at him and smiled, though there was no joy in his eyes. The smile came because Kristoff was beginning to understand the role.

"Can you make it stop?" cried Kristoff.

"It will become easier in time," the figure responded in a measured tone. "For now, I will silence them so we can talk." With a wave of his hand, the whispers lowered to a faint trickle, and Kristoff relaxed slightly.

As the sound lessened, Kristoff's attention turned back to the pillar. It stood six feet tall and appeared smooth from a distance. Up close, however, he noticed a finely carved spiral pattern weaving its way upward to a crystal orb at the top, which seemed to hold a swirling mist. Slowly, Kristoff raised his hand towards the orb, rising onto his tiptoes to reach it.

59

THE LAST JOURNEY

Before he could touch it, the figure stopped him, his hand hovering just short of the surface. Kristoff looked at him, confused.

"It is not time for that yet," the figure said, his voice calm but firm. "First, you must understand. The pillar shields the valley, keeping people from discovering we are here, but it also serves a greater purpose. It forms the foundation for the magic that keeps the Spirit of Christmas alive. It allows us to pass the magic along for the next person to carry the mantle... to become the Judge, the scales by which humanity remains in balance."

"How is it decided who becomes the next Santa?" asked Kristoff, his voice tinged with concern.

The figure stood silent for a moment, then answered, "To be the Spirit, one must possess a pure heart, seeing the good in all things and all people. They must understand sacrifice and the ripples it creates in the world. Such a person must be beyond reproach, fully accepting the immense importance of this role."

The words fell like a massive weight onto Kristoff's shoulders. He had dreamed of what it would be like to be Santa since he was a kid – the thought that it was all about flying around at Christmas, handing out gifts to good boys and girls. He had never imagined, even for the briefest moment, that there was so much more to this role or how critical it was for the world's survival. *How can someone listen to all the darkness people carry with them without being affected?* he wondered.

60

A CHRISTMAS MENAGERIE

As if in response, the figure touched Kristoff's shoulder lightly. "People are also filled with such potential for good," he said solemnly. "It is that hope that helps us continue our work. We must become the beacon for them – the desire to be better, to help others, and to carry the Spirit of the season with them everywhere. This is a lot to show you at once, and for that I apologize – there was no other way. Time is short, and you must be made to understand."

As the figure's hand rested on his shoulder, Kristoff's mind raced with images of his time here. He looked back on the lessons the Spirit had taught him. He recalled all the time spent with the helpers, learning how the castle and village operated all year long, in preparation for that one magical night. Slowly, he began to understand that the figure had been preparing him for this very night – this very moment.

Tears filled his eyes as he slowly turned to the figure. "I can't do it," he said, his voice trembling. "I can't become you. I can't do what you do."

The figure's hand slowly moved to Kristoff's chin and lifted to meet his eyes. With compassion and respect, he said, "My young Kristoff, you have been doing this very thing your entire life. You have seen all the best and worst this world has to offer, and you still treat everyone as if they are your equal. You give without any thought of yourself. You *are* this role, my friend."

He understood the enormity of what he had presented to Kristoff, remembering his own doubts when he was chosen to become the Spirit. Brief glimpses of the life he left behind

THE LAST JOURNEY

flitted through his memory – a mixture of sadness for what he left behind and deep respect for the power he carried.

"It is, after all, your choice," the figure added. "You can choose not to accept."

"What happens if I choose not to be the Spirit?" Kristoff asked.

The figure sighed and lowered his head. "There has to be a Spirit of Christmas, for the world," he said with a heavy voice. "If you refuse, I will attempt to find another. If I fail and the role is not passed on, then goodness will slowly recede. Darkness will grow, spreading to every corner of the world and slowly eating away at it like poison. Once the world can no longer survive, it will fall away. Balance has to be maintained.

"You have been here for three hundred years, Kristoff," the figure continued. "You came here as a child, and the magic of the valley has maintained your age until you make your choice. Though you look like a child, you are a man on the inside. You must weigh your choices and decide what's best. I have taught you almost everything I can, and my time is running out."

"But... what..." Kristoff began, trailing off as he turned and realized that the figure had left him standing alone before the pillar. *Is this real? Why me?* and *What does all of this mean?* were but some of the questions swirling around in his mind, like the mist in the orb. Kristoff pondered what would happen if he decided he wasn't the one.

As if to answer, the orb twinkled brightly, drawing his attention. Seeing the spark, he reached towards the crystal

A CHRISTMAS MENAGERIE

sphere again. As his fingers inched closer, the light intensified and soon enveloped him.

Thunderous noises immediately flooded his mind while the acrid smell of smoke filled his nostrils. The air felt both icy and ablaze. Darkness surrounded him, and he stumbled forward, his arms outstretched. Though it seemed like an eternity, only a few seconds passed before his vision cleared. What lay before him left him in shock.

He stood in a city, though none he recognized. Buildings were either collapsed or crumbling, as if devastated by a massive explosion. The air was thick with smoke, making every breath painful. All around him, he heard the sounds of distant explosions mixed with people screaming – some screams of pain and others filled with rage. The world was in shambles, as if the very stitches of its foundation had been loosened.

Kristoff's mind raced with fear. *What caused this? What can I do?* The world felt utterly lost, devoid of love and compassion. "How did this happen?" he muttered. Suddenly, a memory echoed through his mind: *"There has to be a Spirit of Christmas, for the world."*

With that, the vision faded, and Kristoff found himself back in the room where it all began, his legs unsteady beneath him. Grasping the magnitude of his decision, he abruptly turned, left the chambers, and darted down the hall. His pace quickened with each step until he was practically running, arms outstretched to push through the castle's front doors. The heavy

THE LAST JOURNEY

doors resisted for only a moment before swinging open, allowing him to step out into the frosty air.

Blinding sunlight reflected off the snow as Kristoff slid to a stop. As his senses returned, he welcomed the joyful clamor around him — a stark contrast to the dreadful cacophony that lingered in his mind from the pillar. His gaze drifted past the brightly painted village surrounding the castle to the frozen lake beyond, then to the pine forest stretching into the distance. Slowly turning in a circle, he took in the sweeping vistas of the mountains that encircled the castle on three sides. Their towering peaks formed a natural funnel, carrying every child's wishes — and their deepest, most hidden feelings — to Santa. They all came here to be heard and judged by the Spirit.

As he finished his circle, Kristoff was struck by a profound realization: this was his true home — the place where he felt safest. The only time he had felt this secure was beside his parents when they were still alive. He knew he could live nowhere else, yet he doubted he could do what was asked of him. How could *he* be Santa? He came from nothing — no position of power or influence. How could he possibly make a difference? A deep sadness washed over him as the full meaning of the figure's words sank in. Without the Spirit of Christmas, there would be no Santa, no village, no childhood dreams — and no world.

"It is those very feelings that show you are the right choice," the figure said softly. Kristoff was startled, realizing the figure had been standing just behind him. "Above all others, you understand the gravity of this decision and its costs. You

64

A CHRISTMAS MENAGERIE

don't seek this role; instead, you question your worth. That humility will afford you the compassion needed to choose the fate of the children you encounter."

"I understand, Santa," Kristoff said, looking up at him. "But this job... it's too much to ask of one person. How can I judge those I do not know?"

"You are correct – it is too hard a job for one person," the figure replied. "But the Spirit is not a person; it is something more. That 'something more' will give you the strength to carry this burden. The Spirit will allow you to see into a child and understand who they are and what they have done. Their memories will become your own."

Kristoff stood silently for a moment as the figure's words lingered in his mind. Exhaling deeply, he straightened as if bracing himself for what lay ahead. The impossibility of the task pressed heavily on his chest, yet it was nothing compared to the sinking dread that gripped him at the thought of a world without Santa. Fighting the urge to talk himself out of the decision, he gave a slow, resolute nod.

"It is settled, then," the figure said in a steady voice as though offering Kristoff some of his certainty.

Kristoff's head lifted, his brows knitting together. "But... but I have so many questions," he protested.

"Those will be answered in time," the figure assured him. "You have a year to prepare and learn what lies ahead. The Spirit will guide you as it has guided me. For now, trust in the process."

65

THE LAST JOURNEY

Kristoff gazed off in thought, uncertainty still gnawing at the edges of his mind. "A year?" he murmured as though testing the idea aloud.

"A year," the figure repeated with a calming confidence. "For now, we must get ready for the ceremony." With that, he led Kristoff back through the front doors and into the castle.

Later that day, back in the ancient chamber, the council of helpers stood in a solemn circle around the dais, their eyes fixed on the pillar at its center. The figure led Kristoff forward, guiding him to one side of the dais before taking his place on the opposite side. He patiently explained the necessary steps, speaking with deliberate clarity as he taught Kristoff the words he would need to repeat. Kristoff mouthed them under his breath, testing their rhythm and weight until they felt natural. With a slight nod of encouragement from the figure, they placed their hands on opposite sides of the pillar, fixed their gaze on the orb at its top, and spoke in unison: "Joulun Henkeä."

For a moment that stretched unbearably long, nothing happened. Kristoff's stomach twisted with doubt as he wondered if the pillar had deemed him unworthy. Just as he opened his mouth to speak, a jolt like electricity coursed up his arm, causing the fine hairs to stand on end. The sensation washed over him as he noticed a faint glow emanating from his body. His focus shifted to the pillar, which seemed to shrink before his eyes – once rising above him, it now stood several inches shorter. Then, without warning, a brilliant golden light erupted from the orb, flooding the chamber. The elders

A CHRISTMAS MENAGERIE

shielded their eyes as the dazzling glow silhouetted their forms. And just as suddenly as it began, it was over.

"I don't feel any diff..." started Kristoff, but he stopped abruptly. He did not recognize his voice – it was deeper, stronger. He lifted an arm in shock and noticed that it was different as well. Confused, he wondered if his eyes were playing tricks on him. When he peered around the stone, he saw a man stooped over, holding a staff. Long, fine, white hair streamed from his head, and a stringy white beard hung from his chin. Kristoff had never seen anyone this old before. "Santa?" he cried.

"Not any longer," the old man replied, his voice weary but kind. "You are now that Spirit of Christmas, Kristoff."

Kristoff stared at him, struggling to comprehend. He took a step towards the old man but stumbled, his legs unsteady and strangely unfamiliar. Looking down, he noticed that his feet were larger than before. Confusion swirled in his mind as he tried to process what had just happened.

"It will clear in time," the old man said. "But first, we need to get you some clothes." He motioned to the nearest helper, who stepped forward carrying a bundle of clothing. Only then did Kristoff realize he had been standing there naked. He accepted the clothes without hesitation and hastily dressed.

Once Kristoff finished dressing, the old man nodded with quiet approval. "Now, your training can begin," he said, his voice conveying a sense of purpose. He gestured for Kristoff to follow, leading him out of the room and back to the desk. He

67

THE LAST JOURNEY

placed a large, antique, leather-bound book in front of him, explaining that he would need to read it and refer to it constantly. Kristoff opened the book and began leafing through the pages as the old man shared knowledge as old as time.

The days blended into weeks, and the weeks into months, until the moment of truth finally arrived. A year's worth of training had led to this very night. The old man had left the castle, making his home in the surrounding village, and Kristoff had fully stepped into his role as the Spirit of Christmas. Despite his lingering nerves, he understood the necessity of his new role and the impact it had on the world. Standing on the roof of his first stop, he swallowed hard and thought, *It's time to get to work.*

As he approached the chimney, he dragged the sacks across the roof but quickly stopped, realizing the noise they might cause. Down the chimney he went, emerging into the room below. Slowly standing to his full height, he noticed the tree before him. Dark red garland, the color of pomegranates, encircled the limbs, which were covered in ornaments bearing pictures of the family's childhood memories.

On top of the tree was a Santa dressed in the finest Laplander garb, including a long, flowing red robe trimmed with the finest brown coyote fur. His boots were black as midnight on the winter solstice, and his pine-green pants complemented a red shirt adorned with shiny black buttons and a soft white fur collar. His face was framed by a curly beard as white as freshly fallen snow, and a red Santa hat trimmed in the same fur as his robe sat atop his head. He held a staff topped

68

A CHRISTMAS MENAGERIE

with a lantern in his right hand while his left hand gently rested on a reindeer seated at his side. As the figure took in the sight of the tree topper, he uttered a soft "Ho, Ho, Ho."

On a table, he spied a note from a child:

Dear Santa,
Here is a small snack for your journey tonight.
I have been a really good boy this year.
Enjoy the cookies.
Merry Christmas and love,
Henry
P.S. I really would love a bike for Christmas.

As he held the letter and read its contents, images of young Henry flooded into his mind. A torrent of emotions surged through him as he saw in vivid detail all that Henry had done and was capable of. He pulled his sack close, peering inside and moving the contents around, as if looking for something in particular. Hearing a noise from upstairs, he stopped briefly to listen, then continued his work.

The figure grinned widely as Henry finally made his way into the room and turned towards him when the boy exclaimed, "Santa?" Henry's face was etched with confusion for a moment before shifting to abject horror. He was unsure exactly what Henry was seeing – his vision was his own – but he knew it wasn't good.

69

THE LAST JOURNEY

Slowly, he stretched out an arm towards Henry. As his hand touched the boy, a torrent of thoughts flooded Henry's young mind, showing him all the dreadful things he had done throughout the year. Each memory caused Henry's heart to sink further into his stomach. In that moment, Henry realized his fate was sealed.

Looking up, Henry caught the eyes of the figure before him, but he had no words. The last thing he heard was the drawn-out, thundering voice of the figure rumbling, "Baaaaaad boy." Reaching into his sack, the figure pulled out a small iron orb shaped like a bell and held it in front of Henry's eyes. The room was suddenly bathed in a brilliant golden light, which vanished just as quickly as it appeared.

The figure climbed back to the sleigh, momentarily reflecting that he had just collected his first bad soul. With a deep, chuckling "Ho! Ho! Ho!" he whipped the reins, and the sleigh took to the night sky. Slowly, it rose until it disappeared into the clouds and off to the next house.

Made in the USA
Columbia, SC
21 October 2025

71159003R00049